BAD HABITS!

(or
The Taming
of
Lucretzia Crum)
by
Babette Cole

PUFFIN

HAMISH HAMILTON

BAD HABITS!

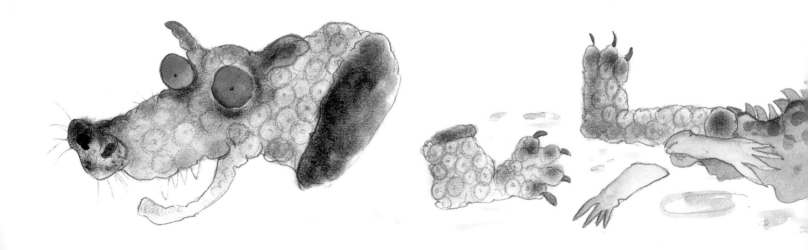

(or

The Taming

of

Lucretzia Crum)

by

Babette Cole

Lucretzia Crum was an uncivilized little monster!

She had disgustingly bad habits like . . .

BURPING

FARTING

and

SPITTING!

She swore

at her parents

and kicked and screamed if she
could not get her own way.

She refused to eat at mealtimes, saying she preferred to starve rather than eat anything her parents cooked.

Then she'd stuff herself with chocolates until she felt sick!

She stole from babies!

She pulled little girls'

pigtails!

The worst thing was that her school-friends began to copy her. They thought it was dead cool to be a little monster like Lucretzia Crum!

"For goodness' sake keep your daughter under control!"
said the other parents
to her mum and dad.

Luckily, Mr Crum was
a mad scientist.

So he set to work . . .

He made his daughter the
'Blowfart Inhaler Suit'.

The 'Burp-bung'.

The 'No Scream/Kick Tube'.

The 'Thief-proof Pullover'.

And . . .

the 'Pull-and-wash Pigtail Doll'.

The
'Anti-foul-mouth Soap',

'Spitting Cobra Ice Cream'

and the 'Classroom Pacifier'!

But as soon as her dad's inventions had been removed,
she became wilder than ever.

Even the cobra left home!

"It's my birthday soon and I want a party!"
demanded Lucretzia.
"Of course, dear," said her parents.
"We'll arrange *everything*!"

All the other little monsters turned up for the party and trashed the house.

Then there was a knock at the door and . . .

. . . some really big monsters burst in! They wrecked the party. They spat, screamed, kicked, farted, vomited and smelt far worse than the little monsters!

Lucretzia and her friends were scared.
"Who are they?" whined Lucretzia.

"Well," sighed her parents, "they were children once, but they turned into monsters because they grew up doing what you do!"

When the monsters had eaten all the party food, they left, taking all Lucretzia's presents with them!

"We don't want to be a monster like you, Lucretzia Crum,"
said her friends, "if that's what happens to us!"

"Well, neither do I!"
wailed Lucretzia.

Mr and Mrs Crum were so pleased that they phoned the other parents to tell them the good news.

But they were having their own party, because their
monster trick had worked so well!

And Lucretzia Crum became

a civilized little angel!

HAMISH HAMILTON/PUFFIN

Published by the Penguin Group
Penguin Books Ltd, 27 Wrights Lane, London W8 5TZ, England
Penguin Putnam Inc., 375 Hudson Street, New York, New York 10014, USA
Penguin Books Australia Ltd, Ringwood, Victoria, Australia
Penguin Books Canada Ltd, 10 Alcorn Avenue, Toronto, Ontario, Canada M4V 3B2
Penguin Books (NZ) Ltd, Private Bag 102902, NSMC, Auckland, New Zealand

On the worldwide web at: www.penguin.com

Penguin Books Ltd, Registered Offices: Harmondsworth, Middlesex, England

First published by Hamish Hamilton Ltd 1998
1 3 5 7 9 10 8 6 4 2

Published in Puffin Books 1999
1 3 5 7 9 10 8 6 4 2

Copyright © Babette Cole, 1998

Set in Monotype Baskerville

Made and printed in Italy by Printer Trento srl

British Library Cataloguing in Publication Data
A CIP catalogue record for this book is available from the British Library

ISBN 0–241–13979–1 Hardback
ISBN 0–140–56451–9 Paperback